East of the Sun & West of the Moon

WRITTEN AND ILLUSTRATED BY MERCER MAYER

East of the Sun & West of the Moon

ALADDIN BOOKS
MACMILLAN PUBLISHING COMPANY NEW YORK
COLLIER MACMILLAN PUBLISHERS LONDON

Aladdin Books
Macmillan Publishing Company
866 Third Avenue, New York, NY 10022
Collier Macmillan Canada, Inc.

First Aladdin Books edition 1987
Printed in the United States of America

A hardcover edition of *East of the Sun & West of the Moon* is available
from Four Winds Press, Macmillan Publishing Company.

10   9   8   7   6   5   4   3   2   1

LIBRARY OF CONGRESS CATALOGING-IN-PUBLICATION DATA
Mayer, Mercer, date.
East of the sun & west of the moon.
Summary: The Moon, Father Forest, Great Fish of the Sea,
and North Wind help a maiden rescue her true love
from a troll princess in a faraway kingdom.
[1. Fairy tales. 2. Folklore—Norway] I. Title.
II. Title: East of the sun and west of the moon.
[PZ8.M4515Eas 1987]   398.2'1'09481 [E]   86-20578
ISBN 0-689-71113-1 (pbk.)

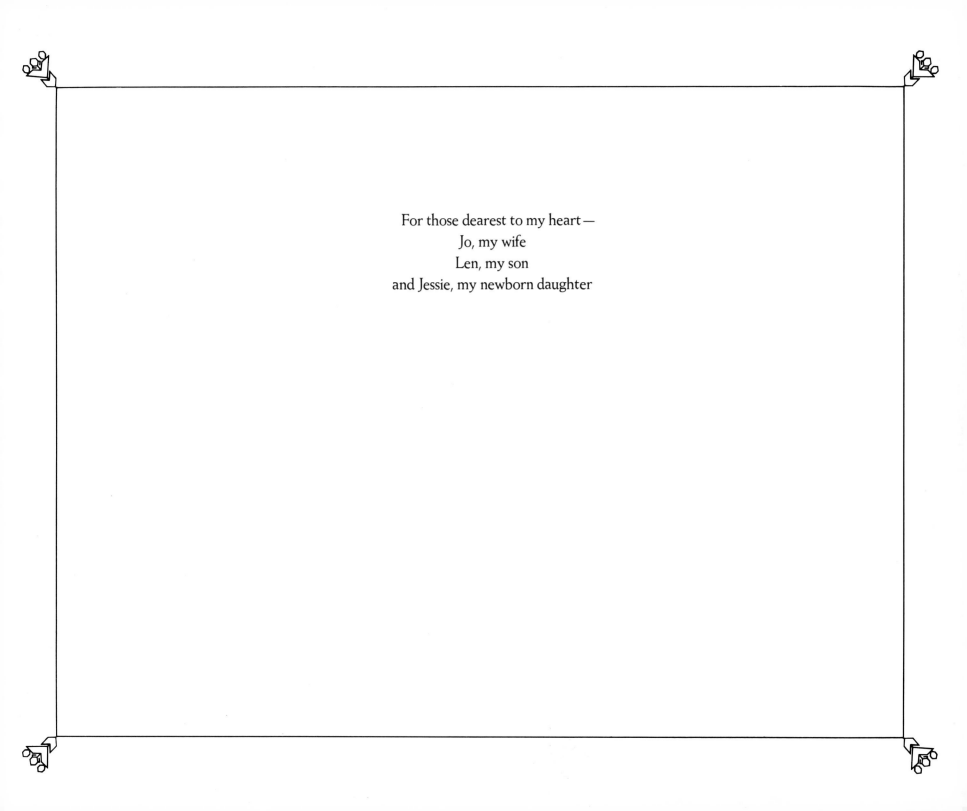

For those dearest to my heart —
Jo, my wife
Len, my son
and Jessie, my newborn daughter

East of the Sun & West of the Moon

Once in a land not too far from here and in a time not too long ago there lived a farmer and his wife. They had a daughter whom they both loved deeply. The farmer and his wife had plenty, and their daughter never suffered any hardship. She had her pick of all the best young men in the kingdom, but none was quite to her liking.

Then, for reasons that only God knows, their fate changed. The king of that land went to war and his soldiers took away all their food and livestock. That winter was very hard. The farmer became ill, and his wife spent most of her time nursing him. Their daughter had to learn to hunt to bring food to their table. Her fine clothes became rags and her hands grew rough. The young men of the kingdom saw her and said to each other, "Not only does this maiden no longer have any dowry, but she has become as rough as a peasant!"

In her heart the maiden grew bitter and thought, "Who will have me now?"

One day her mother said to her, "I must send you on a very difficult journey or your father will die. You must go to the house of the South Wind and from the spring in his garden draw a clear drink of water. Bring it back in this silver cup."

That very day the maiden set out for the home of the South Wind. As they had no horse or ox, she had to go on foot. "I don't know what good a drink of water from the spring of the South Wind will do my father," she thought, "but I will go."

After many weary miles she arrived. But the South Wind was gone and the spring was clouded over. "Oh, what shall I do?" she said. "This water is not fit for my father to drink!" She sat down and began to cry.

"Fair maiden," said a voice, "why do you weep?"

Looking down, she saw a frog sitting on a lily pad. But as she bent over, she dropped the silver cup into the water. It drifted down beyond sight to the very bottom of the spring. She cried bitter tears and said, "I have been sent by my mother to fetch a clear drink of water from this spring. But the water is clouded and I have lost the silver cup."

"I shall uncloud the water and fetch your silver cup if you will grant me three wishes," said the frog.

"I shall grant them if it is possible," answered the maiden.

Suddenly the water cleared. The frog dove deep into the spring and brought the maiden the silver cup. "My first wish," said the frog, "is that you will let me come and visit you."

"Of course you may," said the maiden. She thanked the frog and set off on her journey home.

The water from the spring made her father well, and their fortunes turned again. The king won the war and repaid the farmer and his wife threefold. They had a fine harvest, everything was abundant, and life was good. All the fine young men returned to court the maiden. Indeed, she even forgot her promise to the frog.

One day there came a knocking at the door. The maiden opened it and there sat the frog. "Fair maiden," said the frog, "do you remember your promise to me?"

The maiden let the frog visit her day after day. On the seventh day, the frog said, "Fair maiden, I am ready to ask for my second wish."

"I shall grant it to you if it is possible," said the maiden.

"My second wish," said the frog, "is that you come with me and be my bride."

"What you ask is impossible! I have the pick of all the finest young men in the kingdom. How could I possibly wed a frog?" said the maiden, and ran up the stairs to her room.

Soon there was a knocking on her door, and in hopped the frog. "Your father has said you must honor your promise to me," he told her.

"No!" cried the maiden, "I will not be wed to a frog!" With that, she picked up the frog and threw it against the wall with all her might.

The frog fell to the ground, dead. But immediately it changed and in its place stood a handsome youth.

"Fair maiden," he said, "you have freed me from the body of a frog by death. In this life to which you have released me I must go now to a faraway kingdom and there be wed to the troll princess who first enchanted me. All because you would not keep your promise."

The maiden heard this and realized what she had done. "Then I will follow you and be your bride."

"If only you could," said the youth. "But this kingdom is east of the sun and west of the moon and you would never find your way."

With that, a host of demons appeared in the room and carried the youth away. The house and everything in it became like colors in a stream and vanished. The maiden was alone and once again in rags. She knelt down on the cold ground and wept.

"How will I ever find this kingdom?" she thought. Since her desire was sincere, the Moon heard her and said, "If you travel to the great mountain of ice, there you will find a cave. You will see many horrible creatures frozen in the mountain, but they cannot hurt you. Enter the cave, and you will find in it a chamber of fire. In the fire lives the Salamander. He knows everything that is in the heart of the world. Perhaps the Salamander can help you."

The maiden walked many weary miles until at last she came to the mountain of ice. She entered the cave and walked to the chamber of fire. The heat of the fire burned against her skin. She was frightened, but entered. "Salamander," she asked, "do you know of a kingdom east of the sun and west of the moon and do you know of a youth who is to marry the troll princess there?"

"I know what is in your heart and in the heart of the youth, and I know your hearts are breaking. But this kingdom does not lie within the fiery heart that I know. All I know of this kingdom is that it is east of the sun and west of the moon, and if you reach it you will not find a welcome within.

"Perhaps Father Forest can help you, for he knows everything that is in the body of the world. Outside this cave you will find a unicorn waiting, and beside him a small tinder box. The tinder box is yours to keep, but when you have reached Father Forest, tap the unicorn three times on the left ear and he will return to me."

The maiden rode many weary miles on the unicorn until at last she came to a great forest. She slid off the unicorn's back and tapped him three times on the left ear. So tired was she that she lay down to rest, making the roots of a giant tree her bed. She slept, and as she slept she dreamed that the forest had uprooted itself and was gathering around her. The sound of rustling wakened her, and there all about her stood the forest. "Father Forest," she said, "do you know of a kingdom east of the sun and west of the moon and do you know of a youth who is to marry the troll princess there?"

A voice answered like the sound of wind through leaves. "I know what is in your body and in the body of the youth, and I know that your bodies call to each other. But this kingdom does not lie within the body of earth and stone that I know. All I know of this kingdom is that it lies east of the sun and west of the moon, and if you reach it you will not find a welcome within.

"Perhaps the Great Fish of the Sea can help you, for he knows everything that is in the blood of the world. Outside the forest you will find a small bow and arrow, and a goat tied to a cart. The bow and arrow is yours, but when you reach the home of the Great Fish of the Sea, tap the goat three times on his left horn and he will return to me."

The maiden traveled many weary miles in the little goat-drawn cart until at last she came to the sea. There, looking up at her from the bottom, was the Great Fish. After tapping the goat three times on the left horn, the maiden spoke. "Great Fish of the Sea," she said, "do you know of a kingdom that is east of the sun and west of the moon and do you know of a youth who is to marry the troll princess there?"

"I know what is in your blood and in the blood of the youth, and I know that your blood yearns to flow as one. But this kingdom does not lie within the blood of salt and water in which I live. All I know of this kingdom is that it lies east of the sun and west of the moon, and if you reach it you will not find a welcome within.

"Perhaps the North Wind can help you, for he is older and wiser than I. He knows everything that is in the mind of the world. Jump on my back and I will take you there."

The maiden rode many weary miles on the back of the Great Fish. They traveled past huge ice floes and towering palaces of snow and ice. When they reached the home of the North Wind the Great Fish gave the maiden one of the scales from his back. It was as bright as the surface of a mirror.

The maiden knocked at the door of the North Wind. Her feet and hands were numb and sleep was overtaking her. The door opened and a servant led her to a seat before a blazing fire. "Is the North Wind home?" asked the maiden.

"No," answered the servant, "but he will meet with you in his garden tomorrow."

The next day the maiden waited in the garden. Soon a fierce storm gathered and swirled about her. "Oh, North Wind," said the maiden, "do you know of a kingdom that is east of the sun and west of the moon and do you know of a youth who is to marry the troll princess there?"

"I know what is in your mind and in the mind of the youth. I know that your mind has one purpose and his the same. I know what is in the mind of the earth and of the moon and of the sun. Yes, I know of this kingdom. It is farther than I have ever gone, but I will take you there if you will be brave, for you will not find a welcome in that place."

The North Wind picked her up and carried her high over the earth. Wherever they went violent storms blew and raged below. They traveled east of the sun and west of the moon, and by the time they reached the troll kingdom the North Wind was very weak. He said, "Be careful in this place. Some find their way here but few ever return."

The maiden was very tired from her long journey, but she walked up to the troll castle and knocked on the door. "I am just a girl looking for work," said the maiden to the troll princess who answered.

"Good. Then come right in," said the troll princess, who meant to let the poor girl work until the trolls turned her into a stone statue. "Clean everything in the castle except the room behind the door with the gold knob on the third floor."

The maiden began to work and all the while the trolls in the castle teased her and threw sand and dirt on each place that she had cleaned. When she reached the second floor the troll princess threw soot all around and pulled her hair.

The maiden was so tired that she could hardly move, but she finally reached the third floor. She found the door with the gold knob and opened it.

Before her was the youth. He lay motionless, his eyes closed, encased in a block of ice. Quickly the maiden took the small tinder box from beneath her rags and set the bedclothes on fire. The fire melted the ice and the water put out the fire. The youth stirred, and reached out his hand to the maiden. He had been frozen for so long that he was very weak. The maiden took his hand and together they walked out of the room and down the stairs.

There on the second floor waited the troll princess, an ax in her hand. Quickly the maiden took the small bow and arrow from beneath her rags and shot the troll princess in the heart. The troll princess turned into wood instantly. On the first floor the troll mother and all the other trolls rushed screaming at the maiden and the youth. The maiden took the fish scale from beneath her rags and held it up. One look at their own hideous reflections in its shining surface made the trolls shrink back in horror, and they instantly turned to stone.

Suddenly the castle was filled with sounds of joy and laughter. All of the stone statues which lined the halls began to move and return to life, for they had all been enchanted by the troll princess and her mother.

In a happy celebration, the maiden and the youth were married, and crowned king and queen of that land. The troll castle was taken apart stone by stone. A new castle was built in its place, and a city rose about it.

From that day onward, if any traveler on the open road asked the way to a kingdom that lay east of the sun and west of the moon, people would answer, "The way to that kingdom is hard, but if you reach it, you will find a welcome within."